W9-BAQ-114

PRESENTED BY

Katherine Knezo
In Honor of
Suzanne Addicks
1998

WESTMINSTER SCHOOLS

SMYTHE GAMBRELL
LIBRARY

Why Lapin's Ears Are Long

And Other Tales from the Louisiana Bayou

adapted by **Sharon Arms Doucet**

illustrated by **David Catrow**

Orchard Books
New York

For my Cajun husband, Michael, my halfbreed children, Melissa and Ezra,
and the people of my adopted homeland — S.A.D.

To Nancy, my sister —D.C.

Text copyright © 1997 by Sharon Arms Doucet

Illustrations copyright © 1997 by David Catrow

All rights reserved. No part of this book may be reproduced or transmitted in any form or by any means, electronic or
mechanical, including photocopying, recording, or by any information storage or retrieval system,
without permission in writing from the Publisher.

Orchard Books
95 Madison Avenue
New York, NY 10016

Manufactured in Singapore
Printed by Toppan Printing Company, Inc.
Book design by Chris Hammill Paul

10   9   8   7   6   5   4   3   2   1

The text of this book is set in 14 point ITC Galliard.
The illustrations are pen-and-ink and watercolor reproduced in full color.

Library of Congress Cataloging-in-Publication Data

Doucet, Sharon Arms.
     Why Lapin's ears are long and other tales from the Louisiana bayou /
adapted by Sharon Arms Doucet ; illustrated by David Catrow.
          p.   cm.
     Summary: Three tales of Compère Lapin who practices his tricks among
the Creoles and the Cajuns of the Louisiana bayou.
     ISBN 0-531-30041-2. — ISBN 0-531-33041-9 (lib. bdg.)
     1.Tales —Louisiana. [1. Folklore—Louisiana.] I. Catrow, David, ill.
II. Title.
     PZ8.1.D75Wh 1997
     398.2'09763'0452932—dc21   96-53304

Contents

Glossary

The pronunciation guide is here to help, but some sounds
in French just aren't found in English.

à la mode (ah lah mode) with ice cream

bayou (BY yoo) wide, slow-moving stream

bijou (bee ZHOO) jewel

canaille (kah NYE) mischievous, tricky, shrewd

chatte, la (shaht, lah) cat, also wildcat

cher, chérie (share, shay REE) dear

cocodrie (coe coe DREE) alligator (from *crocodile:* crocodile)

compère (comb PARE) comrade, brother

eau de (oh duh) water of, as in eau de toilette

gris gris (GREE gree) spell, charm, or incantation

gumbo (GUM boh) a thick soup with a roux base

hors d'oeuvre (or DUV) appetizer

jambalaya (jum buh LYE yuh) a thick mixture of rice, meat, and seasonings

jump the broomstick an old Cajun wedding custom

lapin (lah PAN, but leave off the N as in Chopin) rabbit

Ma'amselle (mahm ZEL) short for Mademoiselle, or Miss

Madame (mah DAM) Mrs.

Mardi Gras (mahr dee GRAH) Fat Tuesday, or a day of masked revelry
  before Ash Wednesday, the first day of Lent

mon ami (moh nah MEE) my friend

M'sieur (ms YOO) short for Monsieur, or Mister

parish county in Louisiana

Rikiri, rikiri, gris gris vini (REE kee ree, REE kee ree, gree gree VEE nee)
  nonsense words made up by the author to sound like a spell

sauce piquante (sahs pee KAHNT) a spicy stew, often made with turtle meat

tortue (tor TUE) turtle

un, deux, trois (un, duh, trwah) one, two, three

Introduction

Compère Lapin and his friends have traveled far and wide to get between the covers of this book. The trickster Lapin was born long ago in western Africa, probably among the Wolof tribe in Senegal and Gambia. In the 1700s and 1800s, he was captured along with his fellow tribesmen and brought to Louisiana in the holds of slave ships. There his stories were translated into French and mingled with elements of European folktales.

Compère Lapin liked his Louisiana home, where he practiced his tricks among both the Creoles, or French-speaking Blacks, and the Cajuns, descendants of the French Acadians who had been exiled by the British from their Canadian homeland. Later, he hopped off other slave ships along the English-speaking eastern coast of the United States, where he was made famous by Joel Chandler Harris as "Br'er Rabbit."

Compère Lapin is indebted to the folklorists who collected his stories in various regions of south Louisiana while they were still ripe for the picking. These include Alcée Fortier, who published his first tales in 1888, and such twentieth-century collectors as Calvin Claudel, Corinne Saucier, Elizabeth Brandon, and Barry Ancelet.

While the storyteller's art has embellished and embroidered the adaptations presented here, the stories remain true to the spirit of the early tales. Lapin wouldn't have it any other way.

Why Lapin's Ears Are Long

n the banks of a Louisiana bayou, not so very long ago, lived a rabbit named Compère Lapin, who was forever stirring up trouble.

Now Lapin was clever and cunning, and so crafty he could trick the stripes off a skunk. But what he wasn't was big, and he wasn't strong. And so he wasn't happy.

"If I was as big as Compère Wildcat," he'd grumble to himself, "I'd get me some respect. If I was as big as Compère Alligator, I could take on anybody. And if I was as big as Compère Bear, why, I'd be governor of the whole Atchafalaya Swamp!"

One fine spring day, when Lapin was feeling about as low as a june bug under a log, he heard a peculiar murmur coming from behind the stump of an old cypress tree. He pricked up his ears, which in those days were no longer than a lamb's tail, and crept closer.

There was Madame Tortue, the snapping turtle, all draped in shawls and scarves and Mardi Gras beads. A big book lay open on the stump with a tall white candle sputtering over it. Scattered all around were pots and jars of the strangest potions and powders Compère Lapin had ever seen.

Madame Tortue waved her hands over a steaming black pot and chanted,
"*Rikiri, rikiri, gris gris vini.*"

"What you doing, Madame?" said Compère Lapin. "You trying out a new recipe?"

The turtle was so startled she nearly jumped out of her shell. But when she saw it was only Lapin, she sniffed. "Me, I'm learning how to do the *gris gris*," she said. "Look out or I'll put a spell on *you!*"

Compère Lapin's eyes got wide. "You mean, like magic? Could that there *gris gris* make me big?"

"How big you want to be?" said Madame Tortue.

"Big as Wildcat—no, big as Alligator—no, bigger! I wanna be big as Bear!"

"Let me look it up, *cher*." Madame flipped through the book, ran her leathery finger down a page, and said, "Hmmm. Um-hum."

"Can you do it? Can you?" Compère Lapin hopped up and down.

"O' course *I* can. But can *you?*"

"What you mean?"

"I got to make you a *gris gris* bag, and *you* got to fetch me the fixings. They's not easy to get, either."

"Anything, I'll do anything," said Compère Lapin.

"All right then," said Madame Tortue. She licked her finger and flipped some more pages. "Mm-mmm," she said, shaking her head. "First you needs a cup of the milk of a wildcat."

"Why, that ain't nothing," said Compère Lapin, and he hightailed it into the woods.

Pretty soon he came upon a mama wildcat guarding a litter of noisy new-born cubs. She hitched up her back, pulled back her lip, and spat at Lapin.

But he didn't even blink. "I come to warn you, Madame La Chatte," he said, all excited like. "There's trouble in the air."

"Trouble?" said the wildcat, peering over her shoulder.

"Yes ma'am. You see Compère Hawk up there? I heard him say he was han-kering for the taste of tender young cat for dinner."

Sure enough, there was Hawk making slow, lazy circles in the clear blue sky. Madame La Chatte fixed her gaze on that bird and began to follow his swooping loops. She stared and stared till her eyeballs rolled round in her head like pinballs. She was plumb hypnotized.

Compère Lapin marched up bold as you please and milked that wildcat like she was a spotted old cow. Then he skedaddled back to Madame Tortue.

The old snapper looked mighty surprised to see him back. She took to leafing back and forth, back and forth in the book. "All right," she said finally, "I doubt you can do this one. You gots to thieve you a egg from a nesting alligator."

Compère Lapin just grinned and headed for the swamp.

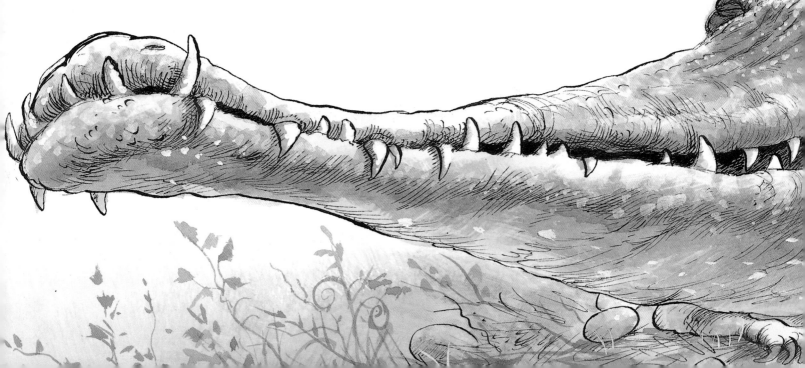

Pretty soon he spied a big ole pale gator setting on her high grassy nest. Madame Alligator raised up on her powerful legs and hissed at him.

Compère Lapin wagged his head sadly. "You poor, poor thing," he said. "Stuck out here for hours in the broiling sun, setting on those lumpy eggs. I bet you get powerful hungry, don't you? And thirsty, too."

"Hungry, yesss, thirsty," said Madame Alligator.

"You're looking a bit feverish to me. Just over yonder by those willow trees, there's a spring of the coolest, clearest water you ever tasted," said Lapin. "Why don't you go cool off? I don't mind watching your eggs for you."

Madame Alligator panted but shook her head. "I mussn't leave my eggs," she said.

"You don't like frog legs, do you?" said Compère Lapin. "'Cause I saw some tender young bullfrogs over there playing leapfrog."

Madame Alligator drooled through her spiky teeth. But she looked at her eggs and shook her head again.

"Well, then, I guess you wouldn't be interested in those young crawfish I saw molting their shells in that ditch over yonder."

That did it. Everyone knows that soft-shell crawfish to an alligator is like homemade pecan pie à la mode to the rest of us.

Quicker than you can say "sassafras," Madame Alligator scrambled off her nest and lumbered in the direction that Lapin was pointing. Grinning like a door-to-door salesman, Compère Lapin grabbed the biggest egg he could find, then scampered proudly back to Madame Tortue.

Her eyes bulged out when he showed up again. "That's two down," he said. "Hurry up and give me the last one."

"All right, all right," she said. She wiped her bifocals, glancing nervously at Lapin. Her tough old hand shook a little as she turned the pages of her book.

"Ah, here it is," said Madame Tortue at last, shaking her gristly head. "This is the most dangerousest task of all. You gots to bring me a tooth from the lastest grizzly bear in Loosiana. He's over a hunnert years old, and ain't nobody been able to catch him yet."

Compère Lapin gulped. Once when he was just a young bunny, he'd wandered away from his mama and just about been had for an hors d'oeuvre by that cantankerous old brute. Compère Grizzly had been after him ever since. But off he went, more determined than ever to get big.

11

Along the way he collected half a bucketful of rocks. Then he filled the pail to the tip-top with red clover honey from Compère Grizzly's favorite honey tree and stirred it all up.

Pretty soon Lapin spied the humongous cave in the side of a mud bank that he remembered from his bunnyhood.

He swallowed hard, then sang out in his sweetest voice,
"Oh, Grizzly! M'sieur Grizzly!"

A gruff voice from inside the cave said, "Who dat?"

"I-it's Compère Lapin. I brung you a present so's we can let old bygones
go by." Lapin set the bucket in front of the cave and hopped back a ways.

Ole Grizzly poked out his snout and sniffed, then dipped a huge claw into the pail. When he tasted that sweet clover honey, he snatched the bucket, emptied it rocks and all into his mouth, and commenced to munching.

Before you could say "jackrabbit," teeth were flying from his mouth like popcorn. Compère Lapin reached up and fielded one in midair, then hotfooted it back to Madame Tortue, with Ole Grizzly's roar ringing in his ears.

"I done did it!" panted Lapin, his heart clanking around in his chest. "Now make me big."

Madame Tortue sat down and fanned herself in the face. "Compère Lapin, I—I ain't never done this before, you know. I'm just learnin' my spells."

"You promised to make me big," said Lapin, jabbing his finger at her yellowish chest.

"All right, all right,
I'll do my best."
Madame's hands shook
as she tied the wildcat
milk, the gator egg, and
the bear tooth into
a red flannel
gris gris bag. She threw it
into the pot. It plopped and hissed. Madame Tortue waved her
arms and began chanting,

> *"Rikiri, rikiri,*
> *Gris gris vini."*

Compère Lapin closed his eyes and held his breath.
Nothing happened.

> *"RIKIRI, RIKIRI,*
> *GRIS GRIS VINI!"*

Lapin twitched his whiskers and waited some more. But he still
didn't feel a thing.

He squinted one eye open and said, "You sure you know what you're doin'?"
Madame Tortue swayed back and forth.

"RIKIRI, RIKIRI, GRIS GRIS VINI!" she cried.

But Compère Lapin was *still* as little as ever.

He glared at Madame Tortue with a frown that would scorch a sunflower.

"I plumb forgot," she said. "I got to help this spell along a little." She looked around desperately. "Here, tuck your feet under this log."

"Like that?"

"That's right." And Madame Tortue climbed up onto the stump, took ahold of Lapin's ears, and commenced to pulling and tugging on them with all her might.

Compère Lapin held on for dear life. All of a sudden, he felt a *stre-e-etch!* in his ears and heard a *splash!* behind him.

Madame Tortue had fallen over backward, right into that steaming pot of *gris gris*.

Compère Lapin looked down at himself. He was still his plain old puny self. But the top of his head was smarting worse than if he'd fallen headfirst into a nest of fire ants. Just as he reached up to see what was wrong, one of his ears flopped down over his eye. And to his amazement, that ear was so long he could've baited it and used it for fishing line.

"Help, Lapin, get me out of here!" cried Madame Tortue, kicking and splashing in her own stew. Compère Lapin rubbed his sore and elongated ears. "You better learn a spell quick before that *gris gris* turns you into a *sauce piquante*," he said. And he flicked his tail and hopped away, leaving Madame Tortue to scramble out by herself.

So that's how come Compère Lapin's ears are long. He's still just as clever and as cunning and as crafty as ever. But he never did find a way to get big—not yet, anyhow.

THE END

Why Lapin's Tail Is Short

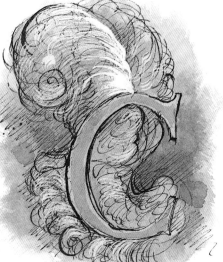

ompère Lapin was as canaille as they come. He loved nothing better than to hoodwink and to hornswoggle his friends.

In the old days, Lapin had a tail that was longer than a bull snake, fluffier than a mimosa blossom, and whiter than the pearly gates of heaven. His posterior was so handsome, in fact, that he was inclined to boast about it.

If he ran into Compère Squirrel or Compère Coon, he'd prance around and say something like, "I could lend y'all some bleach so's you could clean up your sterns." Or he'd point at Compère Bear or Compère Deer's backside and say, "Looks like a skeeter bit you—oops, that's your tail!" And poor old Compère Possum's snaky pink hindquarters had been made fun of so often that he just hung upside down from the chinaball tree and cried.

One fine Louisiana afternoon Compère Lapin had fluffed and combed his tail till he just had to show it off. So he went sashaying down the bayou, twitching his hind end this way and that. Before long he came upon Compère Alligator dozing peaceful as you please in the grassy green grass.

Lapin strutted and swaggered till Compère Alligator finally opened a bulging eyeball. Lapin flicked his pride and joy.

"Hello, Compère Lapin," said Alligator sleepily. "That tail of yours is looking mighty handsome today."

"Why, thank you," said Lapin.

Now in those days, Compère Alligator's skin was as light and smooth as buttermilk. Lapin looked at that reptile's tender white toes, and quicker than you can say "*cocodrie,*" a prank popped into his head.

"Say there, *mon ami,*" Lapin began, "do you know what Trouble is?"

Compère Alligator yawned. "I can't say as I do."

"Well, being as I'm your friend, I'll give you a dee-mon-stree-ation," said Compère Lapin. "You stay right where you're at until you hear me yell, 'Trouble!' Then take a good look around, 'cause you's gonna be in it!"

Compère Alligator nodded and drifted back to sleep. Chuckling to himself, Lapin hightailed it over to the sugar mill and fetched a jar of thick, dark cane syrup.

When he tippytoed back, Alligator was still snoring. Compère Lapin poured a big dollop of cane syrup right smack dab onto each of that reptile's milky white feet, dumping the rest right between his eyes.

Now everybody knows that the softest spot on an alligator is between his toes. And that's right where that sweet goo went to dribbling and oozing.

Before a gnat could blink an eyelash, every wasp and bee and ant in the parish showed up, swarming and buzzing and high-stepping like they'd been invited to a Sunday picnic.

And they all commenced to biting and stinging poor Alligator's toes for their share of the plunder.

When Compère Alligator felt all that meanness going on in his tenderest parts, he started bellowing and roaring and running round and round like a pup chasing its tail. He'd stop and shake one front foot, then the other. He'd run on a little ways and shake one back foot, then the other. You'd have sworn he was dancing a Cajun two-step.

"Help, Lapin!" cried Alligator. "They's eatin' me alive!"

But Lapin was rolling on the ground clutching his belly. He laughed so hard, he barely had enough breath to call out, "Trouble! TROUBLE!"

Compère Alligator couldn't take any more. He leapt straight up into the air and thwacked his head on the limb of a live oak tree.

When he came crashing back to earth, he landed so hard that sparks flew from beneath his feet. That set fire to the heap of Spanish moss he'd been using for a pillow, and in two shakes of a squirrel's tail, the grass all around him went up in flames.

Compère Alligator took a flying leap from the mud bank and landed with a sizzle and a hiss in the bayou. His poor hide, which had been so snowy white, was all scorched and blistered. It looked as rough and scaly as the bark of a cypress tree, just like it does to this very day.

Compère Lapin gulped to see the change in his friend. "Well, *mon ami*," he said sheepishly, "leastwise now you know what Trouble is!"

"I do, yes I do," panted Compère Alligator, slurping some cool bayou water. "And Trouble smarts somethin' fierce!" It wasn't in his nature to suspicion his friends, but Alligator did take a good sideways look at Lapin.

Just then Compère Lapin's stomach growled. He squinted up at the hot sun and saw that, sure as sugarcane, it was lunchtime.

He thwacked himself on the head. Every last sprig of sweet grass was burned to a crisp, and Lapin had nothing left to eat!

He looked over to the other side of the bayou, where the grassy green grass waved in the breeze. His tail drooped, his mouth watered, and his stomach commenced to rumbling something awful.

Naturally, it didn't take him long to conjure up another trick.

"You know, Compère Alligator," he said, stroking the tip of his long, furry tail, "I got ten brothers and ten sisters, me. And fifty cousins, and at least a hunnert aunts and uncles. Why, I bet you there's ten times more rabbits than gators in these roundabouts."

"Naw," said Compère Alligator, wagging his big wet head. "This bayou's chock-full of us gators."

"I guess we'd have to take a head count to find out for sure."

"How you going to do that?" said Alligator, giving Lapin another sideways look.

Compère Lapin flicked his squirrelly tail. "I tell you what—you round up all the gators and line them up across the bayou. Then I'll jump on your backs and count you."

"It does seem like the only way," said Compère Alligator, scratching his rough old head. So he called all his friends and relations and got them to line up nose to tail across the bayou. Then he swam to the front of the line so he could hear the final tally.

Chuckling to himself, Compère Lapin went to skipping from one scaly back to the other, calling, "*Un! Deux! Trois!*" and so forth.

When he reached Compère Alligator's back, he busted out laughing. "Ha, ha! I don't care a fig about counting you ole gators. I just wanted to get to this side of the bayou so's I could have myself some lunch!" And he jumped for the grassy green bank.

But this time he'd laughed too soon. Compère Alligator snapped open his gigantic jaws and chomped down on Compère Lapin's long, bushy tail.

"Why, looka here," said Alligator through clenched teeth. "I do believe I done caught Trouble by the tail!"

Compère Lapin trembled as he peered around at that big crooked grin. But for once in his life, he'd run out of tricks. So, mustering all his strength and pushing off with his powerful back legs, he gave a mighty leap.

R-r-r-i-i-i-p! went his backside.

Lapin made it to the other side, all right. But most of his beautiful, prideful tail stayed back there in Alligator's razor-sharp teeth.

And that's why, to this very day, Compère Lapin's tail is as short and stumpy as a cotton boll, and why he sits down after every few hops to try and hide it. And he keeps a sharp eye peeled for logs floating in the bayou, 'cause sometimes they turn out to have razor-sharp teeth.

Rumor has it, though, that Lapin's still conjuring up tricks and giving dee-mon-stree-ations of Trouble all up and down that Louisiana bayou.

THE END

Lapin and the Ball at M'sieur Deer's

Springtime was busting out all over the bayou. Birds were twittering, bees were thrumming, and hearts were swelling like the buds on the papaw tree. Down in the meadow, staring gaga into each other's eyes, sat Compère Lapin and Ma'amselle Bijou Deer. Bijou was prettier than an azalea blossom and sweeter than a Celeste fig, and it wasn't long before Lapin went down on one knee to pop the question. He'd stayed awake nearly all night composing some poetry for the occasion, and he was sure it would do the trick.

"Oh, Bijou, jewel of my life,
I beg you, take my hand and be my wife."

But to his surprise, Ma'amselle Bijou shook her head. "My papa won't hear of it," she sniffled sadly. "He's hoping to hitch me up to that rich old Compère Stag from down New Orleans way."

"But you and I belong together," said Compère Lapin, feeling like his heart was fixing to break. "I'll just go have a word with your daddy." And he hightailed off to the Deers' house.

M'sieur Deer's answer rang clear across the bayou. "If you think," he bellowed, "I'm going to let my Bijou marry a no-good, no-count, do-nothing rascal like you, you're crazier than I always thought." And he gave Lapin a boot in his short-tailed posterior that landed him right back in the meadow.

"I told you so," said Ma'amselle Bijou, dabbing at her eyes.

"There's got to be a way," said Compère Lapin, scratching his head. "What if your daddy had some kind of contest? That way I could win you fair and square." Of course, Lapin had his own peculiar definition of fair and square.

So Bijou went home and begged her daddy to give Lapin a chance to win her hand. He refused, and she took to moping around all day, looking sadder than sundown. Every time her daddy glanced her way, she'd heave a heavy sigh and drop a tear or two out of her big doe eyes. It wasn't long before M'sieur Deer's heart melted like butter on a summer's day.

"All right," he said at last, "a contest it is. But if that scoundrel of a jackrabbit loses, let that be the last time I ever hear his name!"

Now Ma'amselle Bijou never noticed the strange glint in her daddy's eye. She threw her arms around his neck and trotted off to decide what to wear to the contest.

The next morning a flock of blue jays flew up and down the bayou.
"Squawk!" they said. "Fancy dress ball Saturday night! Test your skills!
Squawk! Winner wins Ma'amselle Bijou's hand!"

"But what's the contest?" Compère Lapin asked Ma'amselle Bijou.

"Papa won't tell me. But what does it matter—you can do anything, can't
you, Lapin?" she said, fluttering her long lashes at him.

"For you, *chérie*, anything," he said.

Compère Lapin staked out M'sieur Deer's house for three days and three nights in a row to see if he could discover what the contest was. Finally, just before sunup on Saturday morning, his vigil paid off. M'sieur Deer led a heavy wagon pulled by a whole team of mules right into the middle of the meadow. And with a *CRASH!* that shook the earth, he unloaded a boulder that was wide as a whale and flat as a flounder.

"Heh, heh," snickered M'sieur Deer. "Nobody, not even that rascal of a rabbit, can dance dust out of a rock."

"Dance dust out a rock?" whispered Compère Lapin. "Why, that don't sound so all-fired hard." He chuckled gleefully to himself, his brain already conjuring up some mischief. "And I'll just bet M'sieur Deer don't have no intention of inviting old Stag to his contest, for fear he'd lose!" So he sent Compère Mockingbird down New Orleans way to deliver a personal invite.

By noon, every eligible bachelor in the parish was gussying himself up for the big dance that night. Compère Coon scrubbed his face and hands about a hundred times.

Compère Skunk dabbed eau de honeysuckle behind his ears.

Compère Fox groomed his coat till it glistened like a copper kettle.

Compère Possum did extra sets of chin-ups.

And Compère Bear took his annual bubble bath in the bayou when it wasn't even July.

Compère Lapin was the only one who didn't fix himself up. He just lay on the ground all afternoon, moaning and groaning and tossing in the dirt.

"Lapin, what's the matter with you?" said Compère Skunk. "The sun's nearly down and you ain't even brushed your teeth yet."

Compère Lapin grasped his belly. "I'm feeling so poorly, I don't believe I'll make it to the ball," he said. And he rolled over on his other side.

"Why, you been making eyes at Ma'amselle Bijou since Mardi Gras," said Compère Bear. "Ain't you even going to try an' win her?"

"What for?" said Lapin. "Against all you handsome lads, I ain't got an ice cube's chance in August. You all just go on—don't worry about poor ole me." And he rolled over again.

So all the critters—all but
Lapin, that is—sashayed on down to the big
meadow. A band was already cranking out a lively
Cajun tune. Fireflies winked in the trees, and glitter
sparkled in the Spanish moss. Thick jambalaya and spicy gumbo
and sweet rice pudding steamed in big iron pots. And Ma'amselle
Bijou looked so ravishing in a crown of Queen Anne's lace that they
could hardly stand it.

At nine o'clock sharp, after everybody's stomach was stuffed fuller than a
politician's pockets, M'sieur Deer stepped onto the boulder and shook his
mighty antlers. The crowd fell silent.

"Hear ye, hear ye," he bellowed. "My beloved daughter Bijou is of the
marrying age, and we're here to test the worthiness of all you suitors." He
looked around for Compère Lapin, who was nowhere in sight. "Anyone
who can dance the dust out of this rock will win Bijou for a wife."

"Dance dust out of that rock?" gasped the critters. "How
you supposed to do that?" But the sight of the blushing
Ma'amselle Bijou made every one of them pluck up his
courage to give it a try. Every one, that is, but
Compère Lapin.

They drew bamboo straws to see who would go first. Compère Coon got the shortest straw. He cleaned his paws one last time and stepped up onto the rock. The musicians commenced to playing "The Bosco Stomp" in double time, and Coon's feet began to whir faster than a hummingbird's wings. He two-stepped, he jitterbugged, he cha-cha-chaed till his tongue was dragging on the ground. But he couldn't get a speck of dust out of that rock.

Compère Possum was second. He tucked his long pink tail, curled himself into a furry gray ball, and rolled round and round the boulder till he passed plumb out from dizziness. But no dust came out.

Next Compère Bear lumbered onto the rock. He shimmied and he boogie-woogied till the leaves shivered in the trees. But the rock was still clean as a turkey's egg.

Compère Fox did the fox-trot, Compère Skunk did the Charleston, but no one could make a dent in that confounded boulder.

There was a sudden commotion in the trees, and who should appear but old Compère Stag, strutting about like a Mississippi steamboat. "Step aside," he commanded. "It's my turn."

M'sieur Deer turned pale in the moonlight. "Why, Compère Stag," he said, "I—I didn't mean for you—"

"You didn't think I'd miss a chance to win this sweet young thing's hand in marriage, did you?"

And with a low bow to Ma'amselle Bijou, Compère Stag stepped onto the rock. "A quadrille," he said to the band, and he proceeded to execute a complicated step around the four corners of the stone. "Faster," he said, and the band sped up. "Faster, faster," said Compère Stag, and his hooves clattered so fast that sparks flew. But no dust.

Finally his knees gave out, and he had to give up.

Ma'amselle Bijou looked tickled and her daddy looked downhearted. He'd been counting on having Compère Stag as a son-in-law. Just then somebody shouted, "Here comes Compère Lapin!"

And sure enough, here came that rabbit, dragging himself along the ground like an armadillo with arthritis.

"Ha!" said M'sieur Deer scornfully. "So you got up your nerve after all."

"Oh, no," said Lapin weakly. "If no one else could get dust out of that rock, how could little ole me? I just wanted to shake the hand of the lucky winner."

"But nobody's won yet!" the critters shouted. "Give it a try!"

"Well, if you all insists," he said. "I'd sure hate to disappoint you."

And he hauled himself up on the rock as if he could barely move.

The musicians shook their heads and took up their instruments. As they played the first notes, Compère Lapin started to do the bunny hop, kind of slow at first, then faster and faster till his long ears were spinning like a whirligig.

At first a little puff of dust rose up. Everybody rubbed their eyes. Yes, it was dust. The puff turned into a cloud. And before you could say "hornswoggle," a column of dust swirled up from that rock like a tornado in Kansas. Everybody commenced to choking and coughing, and every pair of eyes in the meadow was soon blinded by that whirlwind.

Not a soul could see well enough to notice the grin on Compère Lapin's face. You see, it wasn't for nothing that he'd been lying around gathering dirt in his fur all day.

So poor M'sieur Deer had no choice but to let Ma'amselle Bijou marry Compère Lapin. Right then and there, under that canopy of glitter and fireflies, the happy couple jumped the broomstick. And everyone danced and made merry till dawn. Everyone, that is, except M'sieur Deer and Compère Stag.

Some folks thought getting hitched might settle that rabbit down. But the truth is, as long as there's fools to be fooled, somebody's going to come along and do the fooling. And Compère Lapin figures it might just as well be him.

THE END

SMYTHE GAMBRELL LIBRARY
WESTMINSTER SCHOOLS
1424 WEST PACES FERRY RD NW
ATLANTA GEORGIA 30327